**I Like to Read®** books, created by award-winning picture book artists as well as talented newcomers, instill confidence and the joy of reading in new readers.

We want to hear every new reader say, **"I like to read!"**

Visit our website for flashcards, activities, and more about the series:
**www.holidayhouse.com/ILiketoRead**
**#ILTR**

**Phonics features of this book—cvc:** fans, hat, hop; **cvce:** like, rice; **y as long i:** my; **variant vowels:** food; **diphthongs:** hear; **r-controlled:** bird; **blends:** clack, flap, swim, thanks, will; **digraphs:** clack, duck, fish, thanks, with, wings; **inflectional endings:** thanks, wings; **sight words:** a, for, give, I, me, my, see, you; **2 syllables:** harvest; **story words:** dance, friend.

**Guided reading level: C**

Author's note: The dances in this story are Philippine folk dances. They include tinikling (bird dance), itik itik (duck dance), tahing baila (fish dance), dinyu-a (giving thanks), jota de Manila (dance with sound), malong (dance with cloth), subli (dance with hat), pagapir (dance with fans), and cariñosa (dance with a friend).

# I Dance

**by Diana Rañola**

**Illustrated by Christine Almeda**

**HOLIDAY HOUSE • NEW YORK**

I dance with a hat.

I dance with fans.

I dance with a friend.

See me dance.

I dance like a bird.

I dance like a fish.

To Grace, my dearest friend, editor, and lover of dance; to my mother, who taught me how to dance; to Nathaniel, my dance partner in life—D.R.

For Sophia, my favorite little dancer—C.A.

This book has been officially leveled by using the F&P Text Level Gradient™ Leveling System.

I LIKE TO READ is a registered trademark of Holiday House Publishing, Inc.

Text copyright © 2025 by Diana Marie Domingo Rañola
Illustrations copyright © 2025 by Christine Almeda
All Rights Reserved
HOLIDAY HOUSE is registered in the U.S. Patent and Trademark Office.
Printed and bound in June 2025 at C&C Offset, Shenzhen, China.
The artwork was created with an iPad and Procreate.
www.holidayhouse.com
First Edition
1 3 5 7 9 10 8 6 4 2

Library of Congress Cataloging-in-Publication Data is available.

ISBN: 978-0-8234-5838-7 (hardcover)

EU Authorized Representative: HackettFlynn Ltd, 36 Cloch Choirneal, Balrothery, Co. Dublin, K32 C942, Ireland. EU@walkerpublishinggroup.com